Weekly Reader Children's Book Club *presents*

THE
SUMMERFOLK

Written and illustrated by **DORIS BURN**

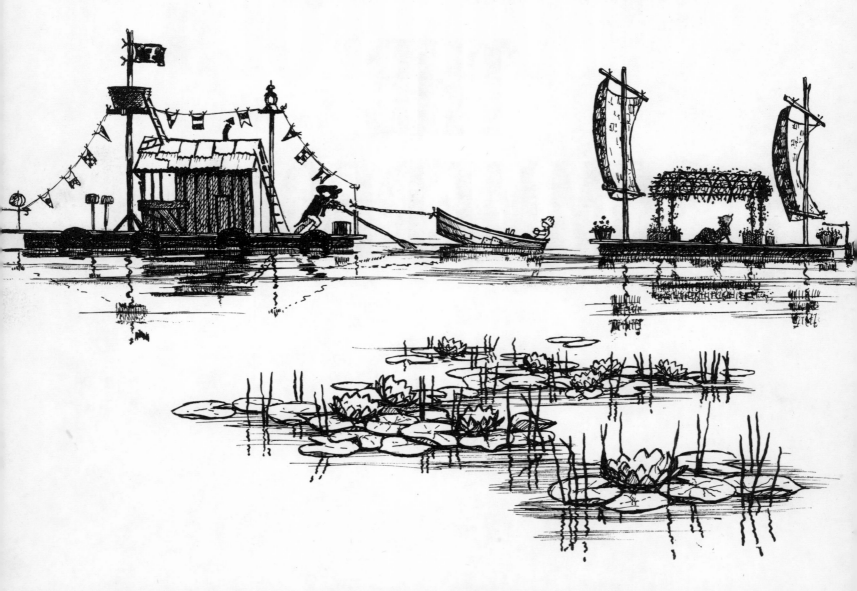

THE SUMMERFOLK

Coward-McCann, Inc.   New York

To the children of the island,
both young and old

Willy Potts' house was on a sand dune. In back of the house was a swamp, but in front the sand led all the way down to the sea. Although the house was little more than a shanty, Willy and his dad, Joe Potts, lived there both winter and summer, for Joe Potts was a fisherman. All winter long, life seemed to go along nice and steady for Willy and Joe Potts.

But all summer long—well, that was another kettle of fish. Every summer, strange people came from the city for a holiday beside the sea. These strangers were called summerfolk. And if there was one thing on which Willy and Joe Potts agreed, it was that they didn't have any use for summerfolk.

The summerfolk set up big umbrellas on the beach. They dropped peanut butter sandwiches in the sand and, all in all, did an unnecessary amount of hooting and hollering. Worse yet, they raced about in fancy boats that were very fast and went Scree—

"Thick as sand fleas and twice as pesky," muttered Joe Potts.

"Summerfolk," grumbled Willy.

Joe Potts had a boat that was neither fast nor fancy, and it went Pop-pop-pop-pop— When the summerfolk set up their umbrellas on the beach and began to drop their peanut butter sandwiches—

"Sand fleas," Joe Potts would mutter, and off he would go to fish for cod in his boat.

Willy had a boat, too. One day he had found it sitting on the bottom of the bay under three feet of water. Willy allowed that it was in a run-down condition, and he did his best to patch it up. He mended it with boards and scraps, nails and paint, tar and calking cotton. But in spite of all his efforts, there was no overlooking the truth. Willy's boat leaked like a sieve.

The only safe place to use his boat was in the swamp where the water was never deeper than Willy's waist. So when the summerfolk set up their umbrellas and began unnecessary hooting and hollering—

"Summerfolk," Willy would grumble, and off he would go to the swamp.

The swamp was bushy, muddy, and shallow. It was choked with wild rosebushes and tule grass and had only a few patches of what could be called open water.

"'Tain't fit for boating," Willy would mutter.

Still he would bail his boat and catch polliwogs in a jar. Then he would bail his boat and catch dragonflies for a while. But most of the time he would lie back in his boat, stare at the sky, and get his head nice and empty, which was the way Willy liked it best.

One summer, on the longest day of the year, Willy was in his boat as usual. His head was just beginning to feel pleasantly empty when the back of his neck began to prickle. And everyone knows, when the back of your neck prickles, it means someone is watching you. So Willy raised his head and peered over the gunnel.

Sure enough. It was someone.

"Summerfolk," grunted Willy to himself. It was a strange breed of summerfolk to Willy, but he didn't let on.

"Lovely day," said the summerfolk.

"Might rain," said Willy.

"Beautiful lake," said the summerfolk.

"Swamp," said Willy.

"Fine boat," said the summerfolk.

"Leaks," said Willy.

"Let's take a water trip. I love water trips," said the summerfolk.

"Won't hold two," said Willy.

"Then we can take my boat, and we'll make up a flotilla, which is fun, if not more so," said the summerfolk. "Would you like to see my boat?"

"Don't mind." said Willy.

The summerfolk explained that his name was Fedderly, which was a new kind of name to Willy. Willy followed Fedderly through the tule grass on a path that was cool and squishy to the toes. Finally, Fedderly parted the reeds. There was a boat.

It had a crow's nest and running lights and other fancy riggings and fittings. Willy had never seen a boat anything like it before, but he didn't let on.

"Might tend to yaw in a following sea," said Willy.

The flotilla pulled away from the tules into the open water with Fedderly doing most of the work, if not all of it. But he didn't seem to mind. He scrambled to the crow's nest, took a reading from his compass, and set a course for north-northeast.

"First port of call will be Rosebud's," Fedderly announced. "It's midmorning and time for brunch, which comes halfway between breakfast and lunch. Rosebud is a great little brunch fixer after she gets used to you. Have you ever been to Rosebud's Stately Wain?"

"Never heard of the place," said Willy.

Rosebud seemed shy and hung back when they arrived.

"More summerfolk," grumbled Willy to himself.

Rosebud's Stately Wain was like no house that Willy had ever dreamed of before. But he kept a straight face and didn't let on.

"Briers is hard to keep down," said Willy.

Soon Rosebud got used to them and began to feel brunchy. She spread a mat woven of reeds. There she served mint tea, wafers, truffles, and tarts.

"What's your favorite food, Willy?" she asked.

"Oatmeal mush," said Willy.

Fedderly got out his guitar, and they sang for a spell. Rosebud sang a song which she had made up herself and of which she was quite proud in her own shy way.

"Frogs sing and muskrats chortle.
Ducks quack and turtles snorkle.
Come to Rosebud's Stately Wain.
This day will never come again."

"Blow the man down," sang Willy.

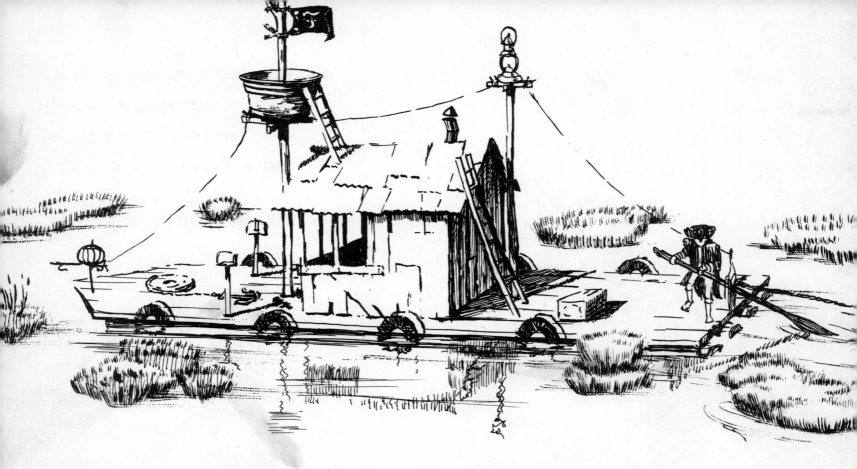

When the flotilla shoved off again, Rosebud's fore-and-aft rigged vessel came, too. This time they steered south-southeast through the narrow passageway between hillocks and hummocks of bulrushes and tule grass.

"Next port of call will be the Green Alder Mansions, home of Cork and Spinner," Fedderly announced. "It's midday and time for a spree. The Green Alder Mansions is the place to sport and frolic, and Cork and Spinner can sport and frolic like nobody's business. So ho, for the briny deep!"

"We're scraping bottom," said Willy.

Willy had never seen the like of the two summerfolk Cork and Spinner. And as for the Green Alder Mansions! Well, there were trapezes and tree houses, climbing vines and bouncing nets. There was a swing that swung from the deep woods into the sunlight umpteen feet up over the swamp.

They climbed, and they swung. They yodeled and whooped.

"Oh, what a lark! Oh, what a spree! Oh, lucky me! Oh, lucky we!"
Fedderly gasped.

"I stubbed my toe," said Willy.

Once more the flotilla started out. Spinner came in his stern-wheeler and Cork in his outrigger. This time they steered due north for the dark, creepy part of the swamp, where the willows stood with their feet in the water and tangled their snaky branches overhead.

"Next port of call will be the Far Willow Reaches, home of Twyla Loo," Fedderly announced. "It's midafternoon and time for lupper, which comes halfway between lunch and supper. It's also time for spinning yarns and telling tales. When it comes to telling tales, Twyla Loo can tell a lulu. Heave ho, for the bounding main!"

"Watch out for that branch," said Willy.

The new summerfolk was heavyset. Her house, her furniture, her chairs and baskets all were woven out of willow shoots. It was shady and cool in the Far Willow Reaches. A watery green light flickered through the branches overhead.

It was a wee bit spooky, but Willy didn't let on.

"Willow makes good fishing poles," said Willy.

Twyla Loo served Willy and the summerfolk a lupper of deviled eggs, rye tack, and pickled pig's feet. After lupper, she told their fortunes with an old, tattered deck of cards.

Then she told them "The Story of the Purple Glob" which swallowed people up and grew bigger and bigger until—

"It's g-g-getting late," said Willy.

So the flotilla started back, and Twyla Loo's house barge came, too.
The sun was low in the west. This time they steered due south for
Willy's landing.

"Toodle-oo, said Fedderly.

"Farewell to you," said Rosebud.

"Stay out of the rain.

Till we meet again," said Cork and Spinner.

"Au revoir and many more," said Twyla Loo.

One by one the summerfolk slipped into the tule grass and disappeared with scarcely a rustle, until Willy stood all alone in the tule grass. Willy felt a little empty, and he felt a little sad. But he didn't let on.

"So long," said Willy.

And he allowed that he might come out here and wait around for a spell next summer, on the longest day of the year.

That evening, as the sun went down, Willy and his dad, Joe Potts, sat in front of their shanty on the sand dune. The last of the summerfolk were picking up their beach umbrellas and zooming away in their fast and fancy boats.

"Sand fleas," muttered Joe Potts. "Thick as sand fleas and twice as pesky."

Willy squinted his eyes and looked way out to where the sea met the sky. He thought back over things very carefully and scratched his head.

"I reckon—" said Willy.

"I reckon there's summerfolk and summerfolk," said Willy Potts.